BANANA!

Ed Vere

PUFFIN

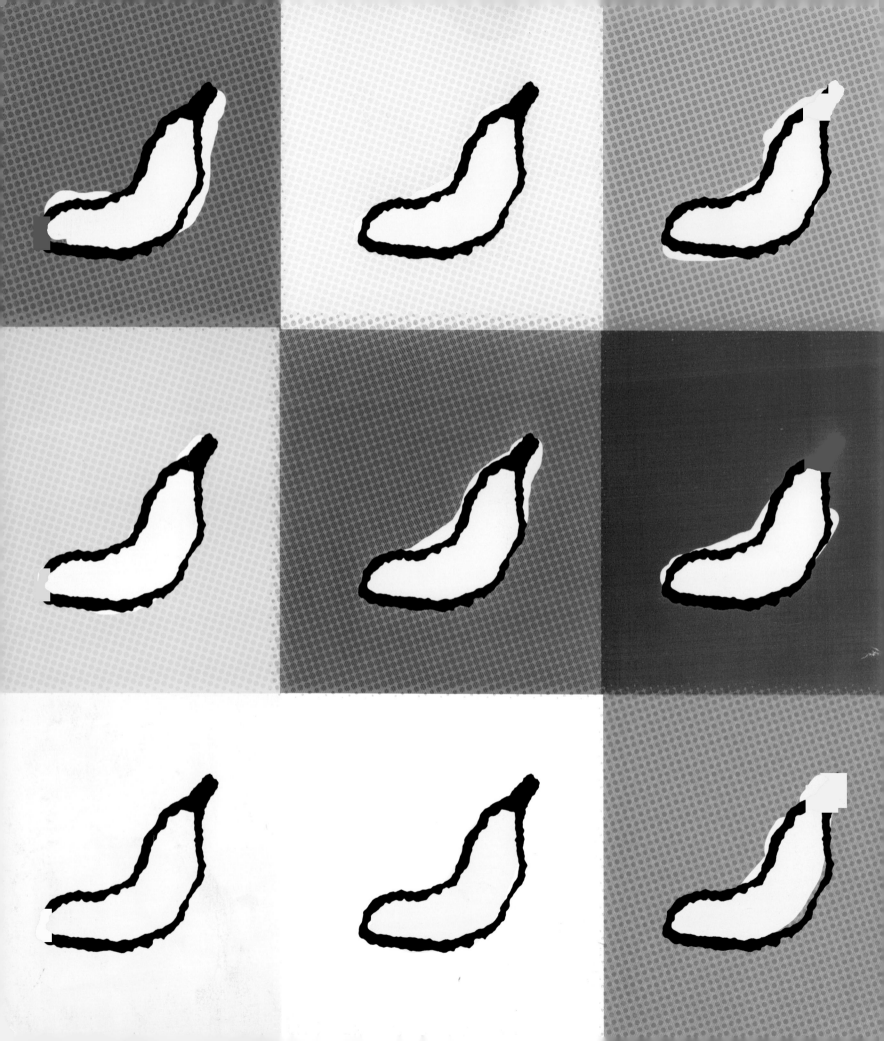

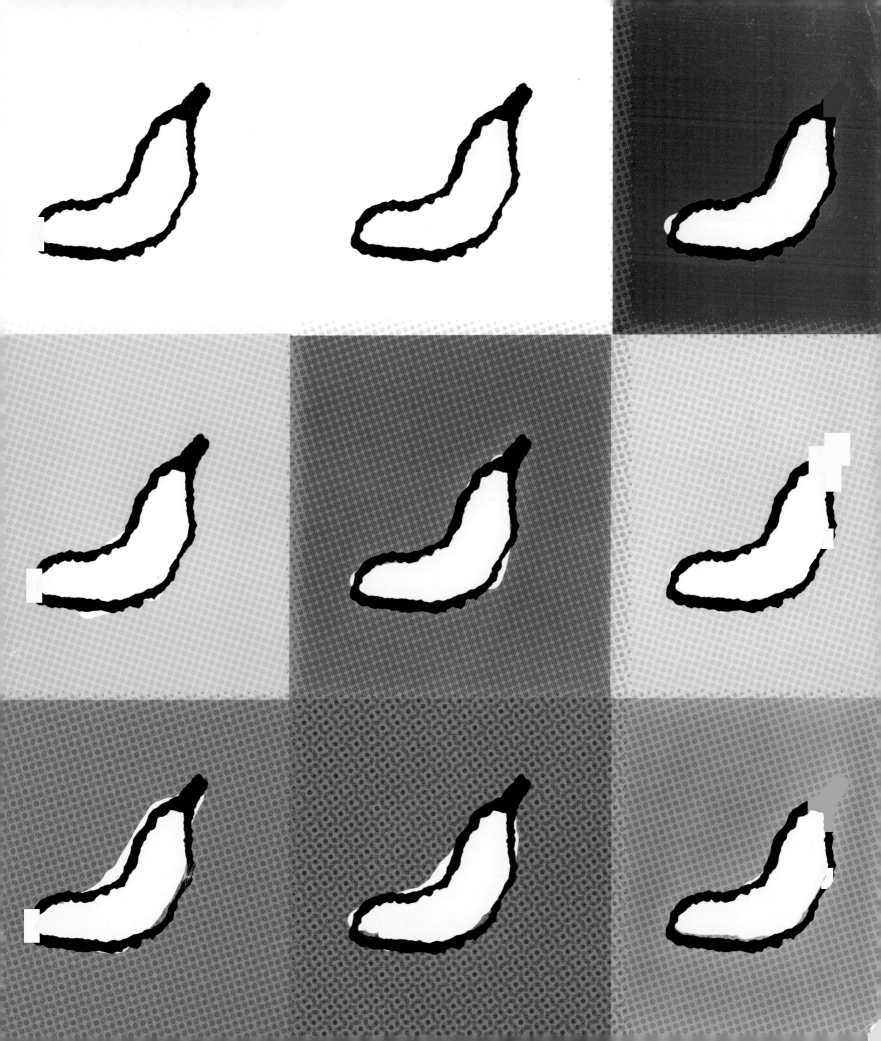

for
Mum

PUFFIN BOOKS
Published by the Penguin Group: London, New York, Australia,
Canada, India, Ireland, New Zealand and South Africa
Penguin Books Ltd, Registered Offices: 80 Strand, London WC2R 0RL, England

penguin.com

Published 2007
10 9 8 7 6 5 4 3 2
Text and illustrations copyright © Ed Vere, 2007
The moral right of the author/illustrator has been asserted
Printed in China
ISBN: 978–0–141–50059–1

edvere.com

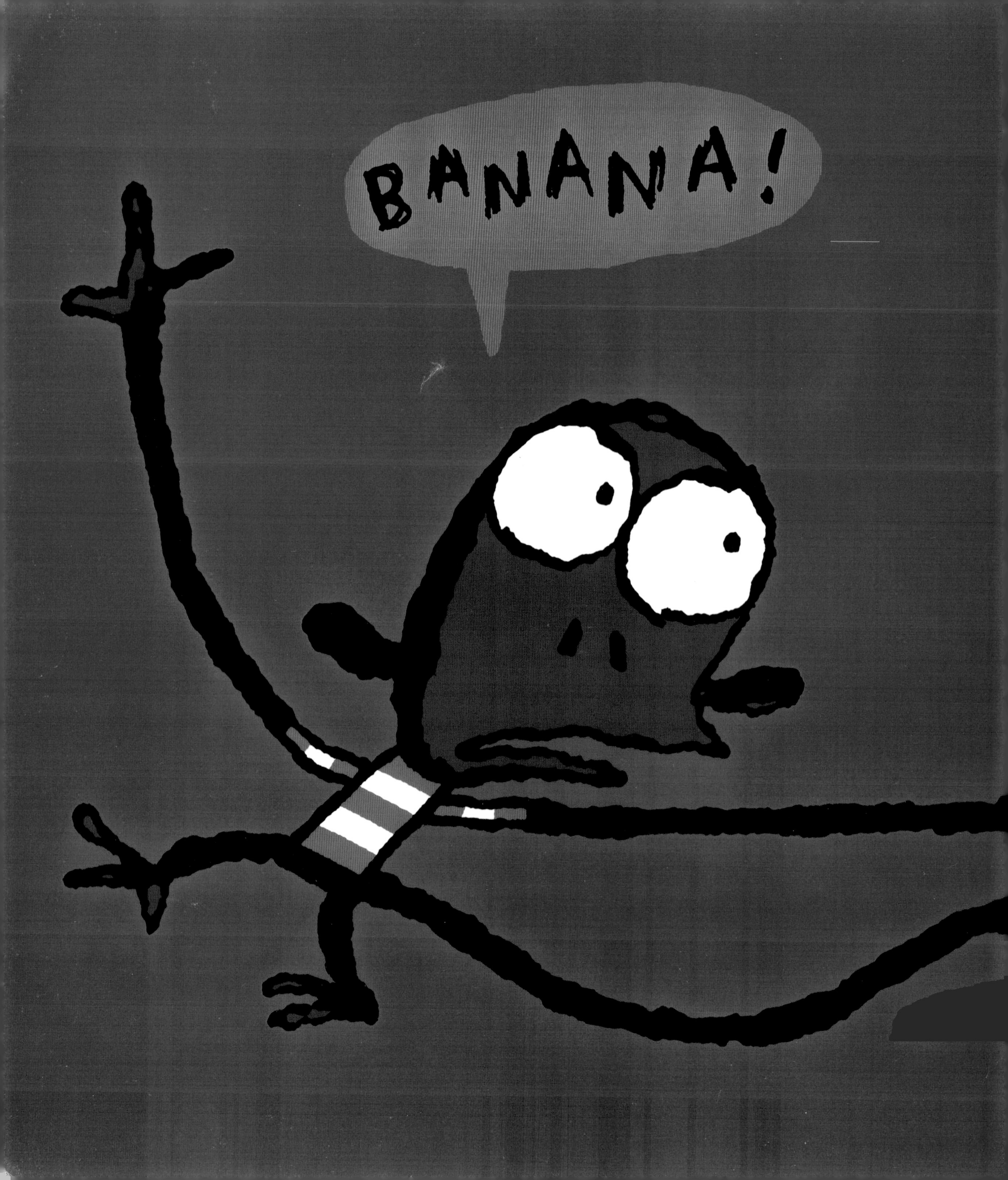
BANANA!

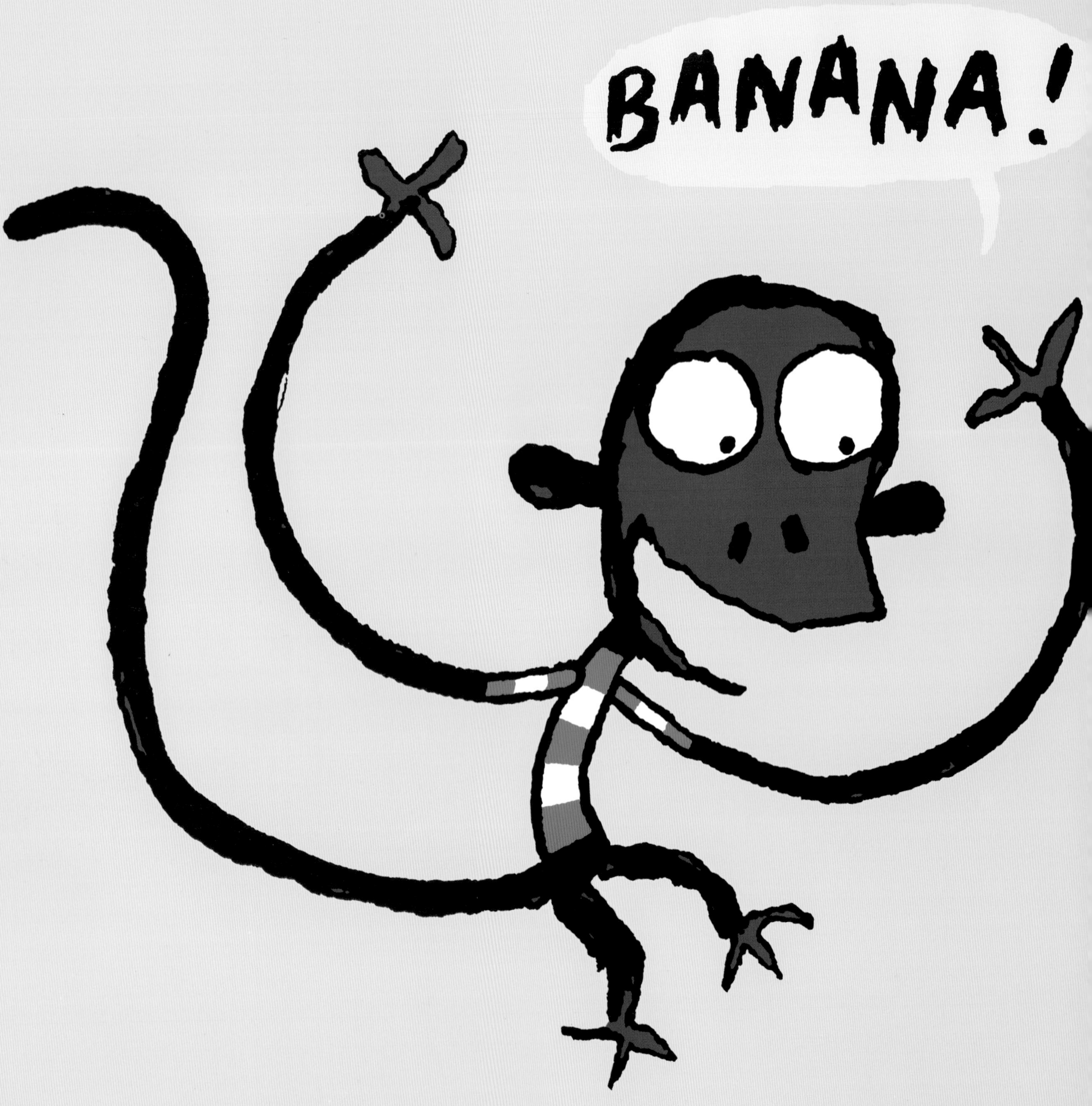
BANANA!

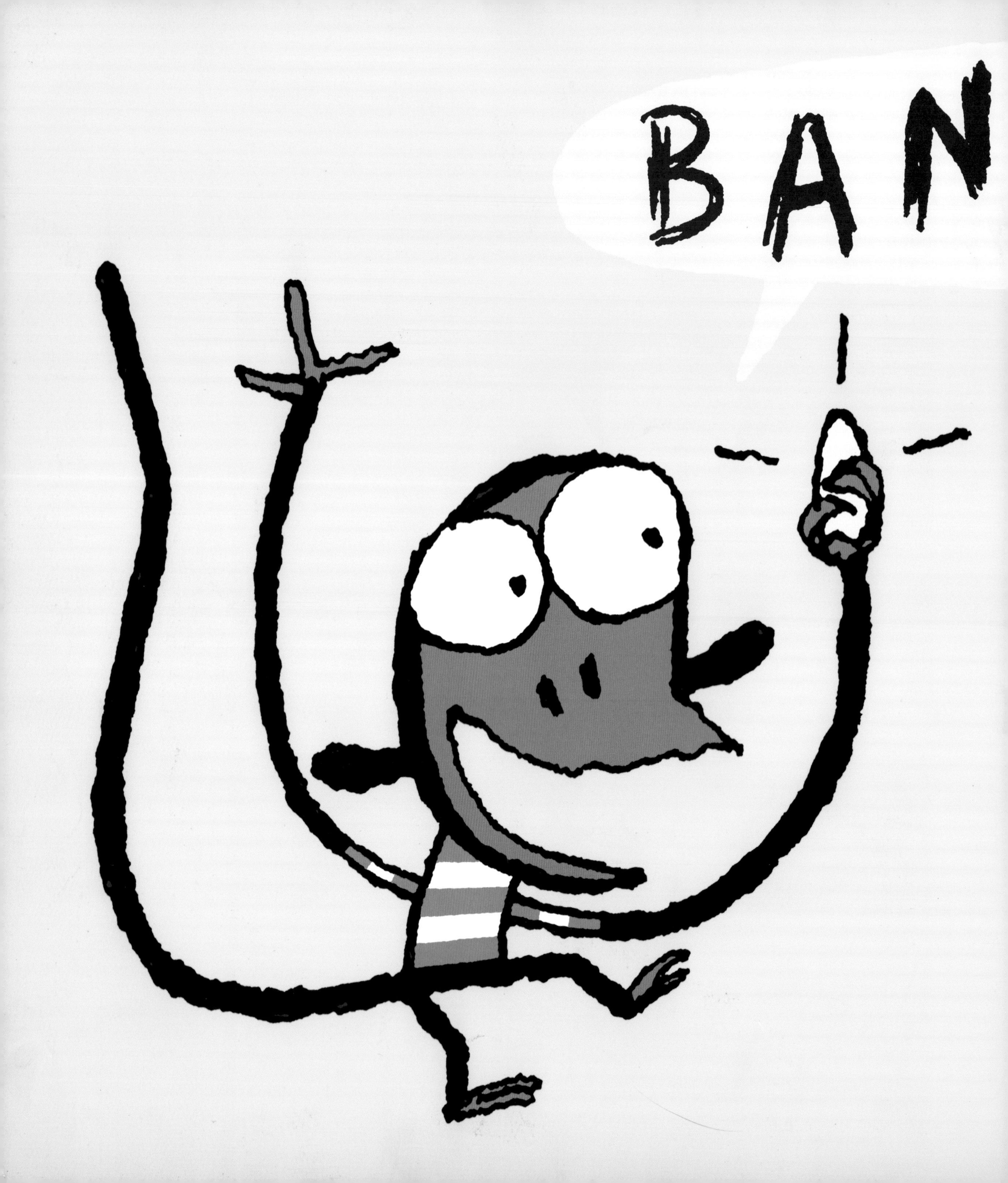
BAN

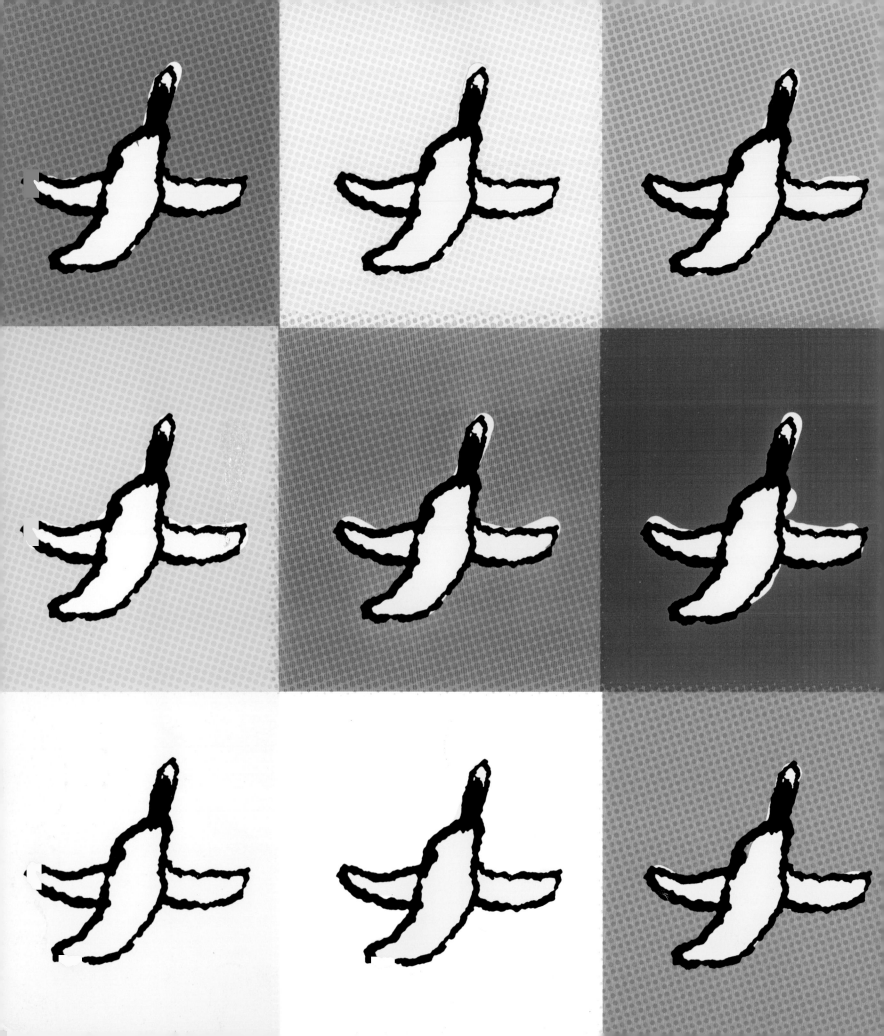

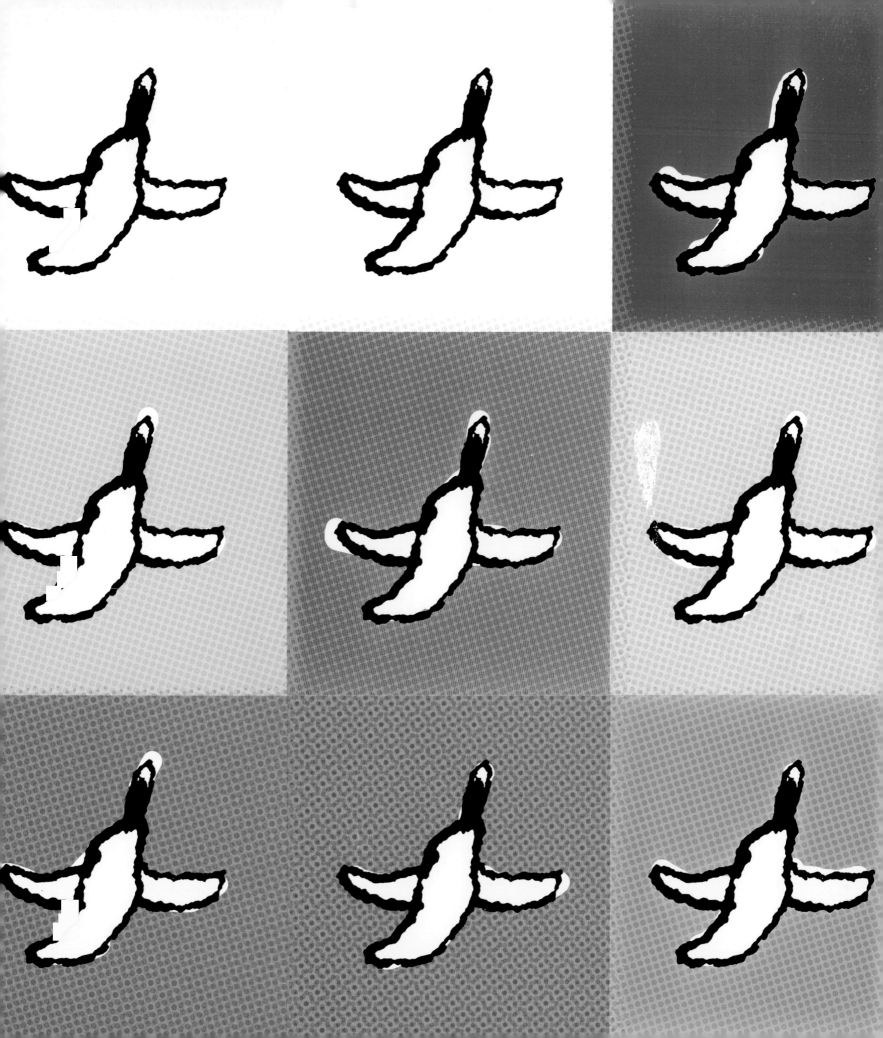